Walt Disney's
Donald Duck and the Garden

Written by Joan Phillips
Illustrated by Francese Mateu

A Golden Book • New York
Western Publishing Company, Inc., Racine, Wisconsin 53404

B C D E F G H I J K L M

Donald Duck wanted
a garden.
He planted seeds.
"The seeds will grow,"
said Donald.
"They will grow into
good things to eat."

Chip and Dale came
to watch.
Chip and Dale liked
to eat seeds.

"Stop! Stop!"
said Donald.

"Help! Help!"
cried Chip.
"Run! Run!"
cried Dale.

"I know them,"
said Donald.
"I know them
very well.
They will be back.
I will be ready."

Chip and Dale
came back.
They wanted
to eat.

There was something new
in the garden.
Chip and Dale
did not care.
They began to eat.

"BOO!"
"Help! Help!"
cried Chip.
"Run! Run!"
cried Dale.

Chip and Dale
did not come back
for a long time.
The seeds grew.
They grew into
good things to eat.

But then Chip and Dale
came back.
Chip and Dale liked
good things to eat.

"Stop! Stop!"
cried Donald.
"Help! Help!"
cried Chip.
"Run! Run!"
cried Dale.

"We know Donald,"
said Chip.
"We know him
very well," said Dale.
"He will not
let us eat.
We must do something."

"We will go back
at night,"
said Chip.
"Donald will be
sleeping then."
That is what they did.

There was something new
in the garden.
Chip and Dale
did not care.
They began to eat.

POP!
"Help! Help!"
cried Chip.
"Run! Run!"
cried Dale.

"Ha! Ha!"
said Donald.
"They will not
come back.
But I will be ready
if they do."

Chip and Dale
came back.
"We will not run
this time,"
they said.

"Look!" said Chip.
"Someone is here.
Do we know him?"
"I do not think so,"
said Dale.

"THIS IS MY FOOD,"
said the someone.
"GO AWAY."
"Help! Help!"
cried Chip.
"Run! Run!"
cried Dale.

"Ha! Ha!"
said Donald.
"They will not
be back."

But Chip and Dale
came back.
They liked the
good things
in Donald's garden.

"They are back!"
said Donald.
"I will make them
go away."

"Help! Help!"
cried Chip.
"Run! Run!"
cried Dale.

"Ha! Ha!"
said Donald.
"They may come back.
But they will not
get in."

Donald worked hard.
He built a high fence.
He put something
on it.

Chip and Dale
came back.
"What is this?"
they cried.
"We can not get in."

"Look!" said Chip.
"Someone is coming.
Do we know him?"

"Oh, yes," said Dale.
"It is Goofy.
And here come
Daisy and Minnie
and others.
We know them all."

Chip and Dale watched.
All their friends
came to see Donald.
They came for a party—
a party with good things
to eat.

"Look! Look at all
the good things
to eat," said Chip.
"I wish we could
go to the party,"
said Dale.

Donald looked at
Chip and Dale.
"I did not want you
in my garden.
But I do want you
at my party.
Come in and have fun!"